The
Flights
of
Marceau

"11/07
To PAYTON
ENJOY

The Flights of Marceau

BY
JOE BROWN

PAINTINGS BY MICHAEL PUKÁČ

DRAWINGS BY STEPHEN MARCHESI

MAJESTIC EAGLE PUBLISHING CO.
CHICAGO, ILLINOIS

Published by
Majestic Eagle Publishing Co.
6649 Navajo
Lincolnwood, IL 60712

First Edition

Printed in Canada.

Library of Congress Cataloging in Publication Data
Joe Brown, 1935–
The Flights of Marceau–Book One

ISBN 978-0-9797495-0-6

DESIGNED BY MARY KORNBLUM, CMYK DESIGN INC.
PRODUCED BY DELLA R. MANCUSO, MANCUSO ASSOCIATES INC.

To my thirteen grandchildren,
Sydney, Sloan, Ross, Duke, Gabe, Maxx, C.J., Sam, Zach, Jake,
Jessie, Cody and Dylan,
most of whom helped me write this book;
my daughter, Bobbi, who restarted my motor;
and to my best friend, Lola,
who also happens to be my wife.
(How lucky am I?)

A new and completely original superhero

Marceau is a New York City taxi driver who, in order to escape from his less than exciting existence, imagines himself participating in amazing, visual adventures which he relates to a regular fare whom he picks up each day for his ride to and from his office.

He uses every-day, adult language, the goal being to improve the reader's word recognition and vocabulary. An easy and convenient glossary is included where simple definitions appear just to the right of the new words.

Collaborators in Marceau's quest to "do good" include the animals, birds and all other living (or not) creatures, the clouds, the sun, the wind and anything else that his fertile mind can imagine.

And it is all in rhyme.

Each adventure is short and exciting to hold the reader's attention and focus. When the story is over, the reader will not only have gained new words, but will understand them in context as well. The tales are entertaining and educational, occasionally focusing on worldly concerns such as global warming and rain-forest awareness.

The good guys always win, the bad guys always lose, and nobody ever gets hurt.

Contents

Marceau Is My Name...

And this is my tale:

I've traveled the seas on the back of a whale
I've flown the sky on butterfly wings
And done many other incredible things.   Incredible = amazing
I've been with an eagle to visit her nest
I've ridden a dolphin high over a crest   Crest = top of a wave
An elephant herd awaits my command
And an eighteen-foot python ate out of my hand.   Python = snake
The clouds have been coaches pulled by the stars
I've visited Venus and Pluto and Mars
I've cured many ills, I've wished away warts
I'm the undisputed champion of physical sports.   Undisputed = agreed

So, Marceau is my name and I'm driving a cab
And my mind does me proud to escape from the drab   Drab = dreary
For the world as I know it is tired and dry
But my mind lets me leap to the heights of the sky.   Heights = top

Now my dear nameless fare whom I pick up each day   Fare = passenger
You'll hear many new tales as we go on our way
We'll play many games with the noun and the verb
And the action goes on 'til we pull to the curb.

Like, one day a criminal was robbing a bank
He was using a one-hundred-twenty-ton tank   Ton = 2,000 pounds
The bees I had trained flew in a flurry
The man in the tank got out in a hurry
His hands in the air, his gun never tested
The law came around and the cad was arrested.   Cad = bad guy

And then there's the time that the church was afire
My butterfly carried me up to the spire   Spire = steeple
I called forth my eagles who blocked out the sun
Their claws carried water, the job was soon done
The people were spared in an orderly way   Orderly = neat
And Marceau, once again, had indeed saved the day.

These stories related are not rare events
They happen quite often and make very good sense
I admit they're not fact but just how I feel
While driving my cab they appear very real   Appear = seem
My adventures are laden with great joy and sorrow   Laden = filled
If you want to hear more … just tune in tomorrow.

The Greatest Show on Earth

Today, my new friend, you'll get full money's worth
As I tell of a show called the greatest on earth
Relax in your seat as this story unravels   Unravels = opens
For I've quite a good tale as we set to our travels.

While driving my cab down the main street in town
I imagined myself as a great circus clown
Not an ordinary clown in the sense of the word
But a clown that works wonders completely absurd   Absurd = silly
Like lifting the strong man who's lifting a ton
Or walking a kite string clear up to the sun.

Old Stephan the lion tamer was a son of a gun
Who thought causing trouble was really great fun
He once fell for Goldie, the queen of the air
Whose act had her hanging by one lock of hair
The star of the show was her husband, named Jim
So Stephan decided to get rid of him
He cut the trapeze, which was left unattended   Trapeze = circus swing
When the wire felt weight, Jim's life would be ended.

5

The band played a polka as Jim was ascending   Ascending = going up
He had no way of knowing his life might be ending
Not I, nor the crowd, nor the boys in the band
Suspected at all that a murder was planned.   Suspected = thought

I noticed dear Stephan standing off to the side
His eyes were on Jim and were bursting with pride
I instinctively knew that something was wrong   Instinct = automatic
My eyes flew to the rope and they didn't wait long
For just at that moment Jim started to fall
And the only thing close was a large rubber ball
I aimed my shot perfectly, timed with precision   Precision = exactness
I had no other choice but to make this decision
The velocity and direction I planned with great care   Velocity = swiftness
When the ball reached its spot I knew Jim would be there
Exactness was necessary as it had to be
For I wanted dear Jim to bounce over to me.

Well, needless to say, it turned out quite fair   Needless = unnecessary
For Jim hit the ball and went up in the air
He arched up precisely as I had planned for the catch   Precisely = exactly
And I caught him quite cleanly with nary a scratch   Nary = none
He had been in grave danger, a roll of the dice   Grave = serious
When he landed he thanked me, now wasn't that nice?

I put him down gently then flew to the spot
Where Stephan had been standing but now he was not.

He ran for his life, that terrible man
But the means used to catch him were part of my plan   Means = method
I grabbed a lasso from the rodeo show
With which I hog-tied that buzzard and took him in tow   Tow = pull
Poor Jim was unhurt although possibly thinner
And here, once again, brave Marceau was the winner.

You enjoyed that, I'm glad, I have lots more in store
I know a story about cowboys, I'm sure you'll adore   Adore = love
There are many adventures that wait to be told
Of King Neptune and the spy that came in for the gold
There's a story of astronauts stranded in space
And a trip to the past when the heroes wore lace
One of a cowboy all dressed in white linen
And one of a preacher that couldn't stop sinnin'.

I'll have a new tale tomorrow as we go on our way
But to hear it you'll have to wait just one more day.

The Legend of Leadwood

My story today, though it seems very old
Has an excellent moral and it needs to be told.

Excellent = very good

In the days long ago, in the wild, wild west
Some farmers and ranchers had started a quest
They wanted the freedom to build a safe home
They wanted a village they could all call their own
When the town was created in that long distant past
A meeting was held so that votes could be cast.

Quest = search

A sheriff and his deputy had been quickly selected
The villagers, then, felt secure and protected
They named the town Leadwood, the founders were proud
In a great celebration, they proclaimed it aloud.

Secure = safe

There was peace in the valley but not for too long
Because, all of a sudden, things went horribly wrong
There came to that village a family named Krill
With Rocco, the eldest, as king of the hill
Eight of his brothers completed the mob
And their wont was to burgle, to steal and to rob

Wont = desire
Burgle = break in

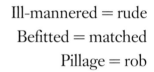

There was Lefty and Louie and Shorty and Goon
Pete, Joe and Teddy and one called Muldoon
They were surly and scary, an ill-mannered brood   Ill-mannered = rude
And would wear only black as befitted their mood   Befitted = matched
They were looking for a place they could easily pillage   Pillage = rob
And selected this quiet and peaceful small village.

They were the meanest hombres to arrive in these parts   Hombres = men
Rocco and his brothers put fear in men's hearts
They walked through town completely undaunted   Undaunted = unafraid
And reached in and took anything that they wanted
Whatever they wanted, no ifs, ands or maybes
Stuff like bikes from the kids and candy from babies.

"Be careful," said the sheriff, "you are certain to fail
If you're not real good. I will put you in jail."
The bad guys laughed loudly, they rolled on the ground
Rocco said, "Sheriff, you can't boss us around
Be careful yourself, we're intending to stay
We like it here, Sheriff, so just go away."

The sheriff was frightened, as you would be, too
"There are too many Krills, I don't know what to do."
When they heard that the Krills were intending to stay
The sheriff and his deputy ran far, far away.

Now Leadwood had no one to do what was right
There was nobody left that could help in the fight
But they couldn't just quit, couldn't pack up and run
Great danger was lurking, life was no longer fun
When the Krills came to town all the citizens ran
It was time that the good guys come up with a plan
These nine nasty men had terrorized the town
A hero was needed to bring this mob down.

Terrorized = scared

A meeting was called, the town hall was crowded
The townsfolk were nervous, they gestured and shouted.
"Who can we get that can handle this crew
The cowardly sheriff is gone, we need someone new
He should be very brave, he should have a strong heart
Handsome would be nice, but he must be very smart."
They all knew the answer, they had heard of my fame
And that's how Marceau got involved in this game.

13

Since they wanted their sheriff to look pretty cute
Marceau donned a nifty new white cowboy suit   Donned = put on
My hat and my pants, even my holsters were white
And my goal was to finally finish this fight
I looked like a good guy, all dressed in white linen
And would now try to stop all that terrible sinnin'
I started my task with a focused acuity   Acuity = clearness
They were right to put faith in Marceau's ingenuity.   Ingenuity = smartness

I went first to the woods where a big bunch of bears
Abandoned, reluctantly, their comforting lairs   Abandoned = left
To assist in this battle and help us to win it   Reluctant = unwilling
And help us they did, as you'll see in a minute   Lairs = homes
A grizzly named Gus was my favorite one
He was seven feet tall and he weighed half a ton   Half a ton = 1,000 pounds
Six of his friends joined Gus in our cause
They knew the importance of upholding the laws
They were advised of the plan and told just where to stay
Marceau wanted nobody hurt here today.
"Just growl and look fierce and wave your arms wildly
'Til I need you, your job is to just stand around idly."   Idly = doing nothing
They nodded and snorted and grunted approval
They were happy to help with the bad guys' removal.

I then went ahead with determined persistence   Persistent = stubborn
I figured I'd need just a bit more assistance.   Assistance = help

Of all the desert creatures that I can recall
A rattlesnake is easily the scariest of all
So, I went to the place where they basked in the sun   Basked = laid around
And asked if they'd be interested in joining the fun
I was warned that before I made myself cozy
I should check with the boss, her name was Rosie
I was welcomed by Rosie in a nice, warm embrace
And she said while she wore that big smile on her face,
"When Marceau asks for help we would never say 'no'
Just tell us what's needed and where we should go."
"Here's what I need, it's exceedingly easy   Exceedingly = very
There's no danger involved to make you feel queasy."   Queasy = sick
I asked that they rattle and make lots of noise
It should put a little fear into some of those boys
There was no need to worry, this was only for show
I had asked that they congregate near the plateau   Congregate = gather
"I sure would appreciate whatever you do."   Plateau = high ground
She said, "Then I'll bring forty of us and not just a few."
Try to imagine, if only you could
Forty mean rattlesnakes up to no good.

It was time, now, to complete the last part of my task
To convince a herd of buffalo to do what I ask
I went to the place where the buffalo roam
To get help for those farmers protecting their home
Ferdinand, the buffalo, the leader of the herd
Said, "We'd be happy to help you, just give us the word."

"I want a stampede but keep it real slow
And just keep advancing right up the plateau."
They thought it'd be fun, a really strange show
Because buffalo never stampede quite so slow.

I sent Rocco a message that the Krills had to go
If not, I would meet them atop the plateau
When they arrived, a strange thing occurred
Behind them approached a huge buffalo herd   Approached = neared
The bison inched forward, the Krills were pushed back   Bison = buffalo
They couldn't defend and had no one to attack.

It was a pleasure to see them now looking around
Seeking escape but no way could be found
With worry in their eyes and sweat on their brow   Brow = forehead
They hadn't the faintest idea of what to do now.   Faintest = least

My plan was so perfect it couldn't improve
At their backs were the buffalo still on the move
To their right were grizzlies, too formidable a foe   Formidable = tough
To their left forty rattlers, not the best way to go
That didn't surprise me, for goodness sakes
Who wouldn't be afraid of so many snakes?

The bison moved forward, one step at a time
Soon all of these bad guys would pay for their crime
As each Krill, in turn, fell off the plateau
The sheriff was waiting with handcuffs below.

They tried to be brave, really they tried
But Pete, Joe and Teddy just broke down and cried
Muldoon tried to run to a chorus of boos
But the growls of the grizzlies scared him out of his shoes
Then Shorty and Lefty and Louie and Goon
Each started singing a far different tune.
"I'm sorry, I'm sorry," was all they could say
As the handsome new sheriff took them away
Rocco soon realized he could no longer run wild
He, too, put his hands up and bawled like a child.   Bawled = cried

The next stop was jail and the judge threw the book
He made them return all the things that they took
The kids got their bikes and the babies got candy
It seems that the whole thing came out fine and dandy
But that's no surprise as I'm sure you'll agree
They had no chance when competing with me.   Compete = play against

Marceau fights for justice, for men to be free
To keep the world safe for both you and for me.

Our ride is now over, we've arrived at your home
I'll see you tomorrow with an exciting new poem
It's a story of mystery, danger and fear
It's one that I'm sure you'll be happy to hear.

The Zombie Jamboree

Good morning, sir, enter, we leave for the city
If your stomach is squeamish it could be a great pity
If you feel you can stand it just give me the word
And I'll tell of a party completely absurd.

Squeamish = upset

There were ogres and demons from land and from sea
Who were holding their annual spring jamboree
The main course was listed as barbequed cat
The salad was made from the wings of a bat.

Jamboree = party

One witch had been talking while eating her bird
Of a tale of great terror she'd recently heard
It involved her old nemesis, the Demon of Kreist
Who laughed when invited to partake of this feast
His mood had been hateful, his challenge unfurled
He vowed to destroy what was left of the world
But if a mortal could withstand his great test of fire
He'd put aside evil, go home and retire.

Nemesis = enemy
Partake = join in
Unfurled = opened
Vowed = promised
Mortal = person

Well, the bravest of men were reluctant to show
But they knew nothing could frighten Marceau.

Reluctant = unwilling

The challenge, it seemed, had more than one part
And each was sufficient to arrest a man's heart   Sufficient = enough
The goal was to enter the demon's dark palace
And escape unmolested with his platinum chalice   Unmolested = not bothered
The journey to darkness, itself, would be rough   Chalice = cup
To acquire the chalice I knew would be tough
To accomplish this feat is all that they wanted
So I began my adventure completely undaunted.   Undaunted = unafraid

Eight hundred dragons were blocking the road
And if one should but touch me I'd be turned to a toad
There was but one fact that old Kreist failed to see
For outsmarting dragons was my cup of tea
My eagles assisted by dropping a net
And I crossed them quite calmly without getting wet
The demon watched closely from a hole in the tower
It disturbed him to see me just flouting his power   Flouting = laughing at
He sent forth his legions of gigantic rats
But they were thwarted directly by my army of cats.   Thwarted = blocked

I entered the fortress with no thought to stop
And knew I must now reach the room at the top
The stairs were in blackness with no sign of day
But my fireflies happily lighted my way
The demon, it seems, had not lost his cunning   Cunning = smartness
He picked up the chalice and started in running.

I took up the chase, I must catch him somehow
And I knew, in my heart, I could not fail now
The demon of Kreist had to cross a large lake
And Marceau, once again, had caught a good break
My old friend, the sun, who had always been nice
Obliged me quite neatly by melting the ice   Obliged = did a favor
In flopped the demon, I grabbed for the chalice
The demon of Kreist had surrendered his palace.   Surrendered = gave up

The people were safe now to work and to play
Three cheers for Marceau, hip, hip and hooray.

And there's the proof for all to see
The world's still here as it should be
Marceau was called, he did his thing
The sun still shines, the birds still sing
All may now sleep for the world is defended
I'll see you tomorrow, our journey has ended.   Journey = trip

Yankee Stadium

Since the streets are all wet and the traffic is slow
Allow me to tell you of slugger Marceau
The ride will require a good deal more time   Require = need
Sit back, sir, relax, and I'll tell a long rhyme.

Be advised in advance that the bulk of my fame   Bulk = most
Results from my play in just one single game
I pray that you think not my manner uncouth   Uncouth = no manners
I speak with respect 'bout the home of Babe Ruth
It was in Yankee Stadium one sunny morn
Where thousands agreed that a star had been born.

I shall try to anticipate all of your queries   Anticipate = expect
About this seventh and final game of the series   Queries = questions
It was the top of the ninth with the visitors at bat
As I stood in the outfield adjusting my hat
The bases were loaded with no outs you see
'Twas a storybook setting I'm sure you'll agree
The game was as close as a horse to its hide
Since the top of the seventh the score had been tied.

The hitter due up was the great Nathan Katz
Who had hit four home runs in as many at bats
A brute of a man, built much like a tower
His body was massive and loaded with power.   Massive = huge
Out of the dugout there came nasty Nate
And the league's leading hitter stepped up to the plate
Nate was determined, he had to best me
For I, too, had hit four home runs as had he.

Our great starting pitcher delivered the ball
The pitch was his best, he had given his all
But Nate met that ball as we all knew he would
And like all of the others, it was really hit good
Old Katz hit that ball, yes, he hit it a ton
And the ball left the bat as if shot from a gun.

My eye on the ball as I timed with precision   Precision = exactness
I ran toward the wall with no fear of collision   Collision = crash
The baseball was flying high over the fence
And the fans left their seats in a mood very tense   Tense = worried
To have the wind hold it I felt was unfair
So I had my friend blow me high into the air
Up off the ground I was lifted with ease
And I felt like the man on the flying trapeze
I lifted my arm to the clouds up above
And was pleased when the ball came to rest in my glove.

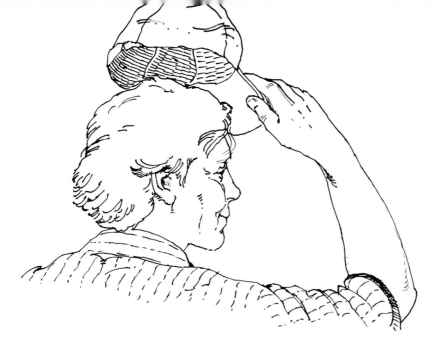

While high in the air, such a beautiful sight
Marceau threw the ball with the quickness of light
You probably think my whole story absurd   Absurd = silly
But I doubled the runner who had strayed off of third   Strayed = moved
Three steps off the base was his farthest advance
But he gambled on Marceau and had very little chance
The third baseman's move was quite automatic   Automatic = normal
His throw into second was very emphatic   Emphatic = forceful
Ben Jones, who played shortstop, had gotten the word
And tagged out the man who was heading for third
I had easily made the best catch of the day
And admit it was truly a great triple play.

★

The applause was thunderous, really quite loud   Thunderous = very loud
And I smiled as I took off my cap to the crowd
You can readily imagine how great the ovation   Ovation = applause
For it shook the arena down to the foundation.   Foundation = ground

My teammates rushed toward me, I braced for the blow
They agreed I had put on one heck of a show.

Now last of the ninth, this would be the big inning
I stepped to the plate with my mind set on winning.
The fans yelled, "Marceau, you must win it somehow!"
And I vowed to myself I would end it right now   Vowed = promised
The pitcher wound up and delivered the pitch
My eyes watched it closely, intent on each stitch   Intent = focused
Wham-bam, you guessed it, my bat found its mark
It was gone, good-bye Charlie, clean out of the park
I circled the bases as told I must do
As the fans shouted loudly, "Marceau we love you!"
The Yanks were the champs, it had really been fun
Marceau could now leave, for the day had been won.

Tomorrow I promise another great show
The taxi will be waiting and so will Marceau.

Moonsmoon

Good morning, old pal, please get into the car
The rear door is open, I have left it ajar

Ajar = slightly open

I have a story this morning, that you ought to hear
It's one of the strangest of my entire career.

Though it may bring me some well-deserved glory

Deserved = earned

I am somewhat reluctant to tell you this story

Reluctant = careful

I've had trouble deciding if I should tell you or not …
But you're a really great kid, so I'll give it a shot
Now, please listen closely and heed my words well

Heed = pay attention

I can tell you a story that you never can tell
It's a tale I've kept hidden way high on a shelf
You must promise to keep this one all to yourself
Let's look all around us before we begin
To make certain that nobody's listening in.

Certain = real sure

It's a story about animals that none of us see
Though they once lived on earth and were happy and free
But alas, they're now gone and I miss them all greatly

Alas = too bad

Have any of you seen a Unicorn lately?

I know you've seen pictures in all of your books
But let me tell you, firsthand, how a Unicorn looks

Firsthand = I saw it

They're like beautiful horses, sleek and well fed

Sleek = shiny, smooth

They have big blue eyes and a horn on their head
For all of their lives they stay active and spry

Spry = active

With smiles on their faces and a gleam in their eye
And what's important to a Unicorn? What's number one?
They believe the main goal of life is to have lots of fun.

Goal = aim, desire

★

But they've been in need of a home where Unicorns play
Ever since Noah forgot them that long ago day
On that day they were busy at play in the park
And lost track of the time and were late for the ark.

Ark = Noah's boat

So they were left all alone, the future was bleak

Bleak = dreary

The flood would engulf them in less than a week

Engulf = drown

But those Unicorns, who were so greatly adored

Adored = loved

Were saved from the flood and received their reward.

Their own beautiful planet, that was as safe as could be
Well hidden from earth, to keep it happy and free
You can't see it from here, it's there behind the moon
It was hidden so that no one would come visiting soon
This place was called Moonsmoon, if you get what I mean
It's a moon of our moon that will never be seen.

There is everything there that a unicorn needs
Like big, bright, red cherries and succulent reeds

Succulent = juicy

Sweet tangerines and apples galore
They have all that they need, never hunger for more
They can eat what they want, whenever they want
Their beloved Moonsmoon was their own restaurant
Wherever you looked, fresh, pure water flowed
That is destined forever to run clear and cold.

Well, I've been to that place that the Unicorns share
But no one else knows that there's anything there
So, it's time for the story you've been waiting to hear
There'll be no bad guys involved nor anywhere near
Still, the problem was one of the worst that I've had
Although nobody meant to do anything bad.

A moon shot had been scheduled early one day
And a crew of brave astronauts were sent on their way
Their target, the moon, they had been there before
But they could never imagine what might be in store
They thought they could get there in one afternoon
But made a tiny mistake and flew right past the moon.

It was the strangest of things, but when they flew into space
They saw this unknown, incredible, beautiful place
They had come across Moonsmoon quite by mistake
Who knew what direction their adventure might take?
So they decided to stop, for whatever it's worth
Until it was time to return to their base on the earth.

When they landed they came out and looked all around
 They saw Unicorns playing and pawing the ground
Running and jumping and laughing with glee   Glee = happiness
As happy as Unicorns ever could be.

But once man arrived it didn't take long
For things to start going incredibly wrong
One of the crew didn't cover his face
When he was sneezing and coughing all over the place
Well, a really big problem was caused by that man
There had never been sickness since Moonsmoon began.

But when the man walked around and sneezed in the air
The flu bug decided that it liked it out there.   Flu bug = germs
Over Moonsmoon it traveled, biting the young and the old
Soon every single Unicorn came down with a cold
The flu bugs then spread with the greatest of ease
Until the Unicorns of Moonsmoon all fell to their knees.

They went to their beds, coughin' and sneezin'
And they shivered all over as if they were freezin'
All the Unicorns cried, they could not lift their heads
They were even too weak to get out of their beds.

If something wasn't done, it would be a shock to behold
Because Unicorns can easily die from a cold
It wouldn't take long, a few days at the most
And we didn't want a Unicorn to turn into a ghost.
So, Ulysses the Unicorn, the boss of them all
Dragged out of his bed to make one frantic call   Frantic = excited
He chose to call Pegasus, you can easily see why
Since the winged horse lives closest to them in the sky
You remember Pegasus, the horse with the wings
He could always be counted on for the important things.

Pegasus said, "I think I can help, so I'd better go
The smartest thing to do is go pick up Marceau."

Well, that's just what he did, and after saying "Hello"
He explained the whole problem and where I must go.

Then Marceau gathered medicine galore   Galore = a lot
And hoped that he needn't come back for more.
Pegasus said, "We will soon be there."
And with a burst of energy soared into the air   Soared = flew high, easily
We flew to Moonsmoon, nothing got in our way
It's amazing how quickly we got there that day.

I hadn't the slightest idea of what was in store   Slightest = smallest
But when I saw it my jaw almost dropped to the floor
In the sky there were rainbows wherever you look
Like pictures you've seen in a library book
I saw fruit-covered branches against a crystal blue sky
And a fluffy white cloud with a tear in its eye
I stood there astounded, my mouth open wide   Astounded = amazed
While a feeling of wonder soon filled me inside
But I had the serum upon which their life depends   Serum = medicine
So I rushed to the beds of my Unicorn friends
Each received a flu shot and a little penicillin   Flu shot, penicillin = medicine
Marceau then departed to search for the villain.   Villain = bad guy

Listening more closely, I heard somebody wheezing
And followed the sound of the coughing and sneezing
The noises were strange so I snuck up behind
But there were no villains for Marceau to find.

38

I came upon an astronaut, her name-tag said "Marie"
She was sitting very calmly, just sipping at her tea
She was so surprised to see me, her tea spilled on the ground
Marie was not aware that anyone was anywhere around.

Aware = knew

★

"Do you know what you did here was strictly taboo?"

Taboo = no-no

"No, I really don't know," she said. "What did I do?"
"Did you notice that the Unicorns have become very ill?
Well, they all would have died if it weren't for the pill.
The sickness was spread by the coughing and sneezing
And the germs in the air that were not very pleasing."

"What a terrible thing," she said, very contrite.

Contrite = sorry

"What can we do to make everything right?"
"The best you can do is to leave right away
And please do not sneeze 'til you're well on your way."

40

Then the Unicorns begged us to never reveal
The secret of Moonsmoon they wished to conceal
Because if people found out that it really existed
The flu might return and they couldn't resist it.
When they realized what had happened, why the Unicorns fell
The astronauts swore that they never would tell
For they knew if they told it would be so very wrong
It would bring sickness and Moonsmoon wouldn't last very long
For the Unicorns there, that would be the end of the game
They would die and be gone, what a terrible shame.

★

Now you've got the whole story, please watch what you say
So that Unicorns will always be out of harm's way
Just remember your promise, don't let anyone know
If we keep it a secret then no one will go …

Reveal = tell
Conceal = hide
Existed = was real
Resist = fight back

We've now come to the end of my fantastic show
I'm so glad you enjoyed the first week of Marceau.
And so, my good friend, I'll be thinking of you
And invite your return here for Week Number Two.

About the author

JOE BROWN lives in the village of Lincolnwood, Illinois, with his wife, Lola. He was an attorney in Chicago for fifty years before embarking on a writing career at age 70. Bop, as he is known in the family, started writing these stories for his children in the 1960s. After retiring he began, again, writing about Marceau's adventures. Now 72, this is the first book of an ongoing series that has taken more than forty years to write.

About the artists

MICHAEL PUKÁČ was born and raised on the Gulf coast of Alabama and now resides in Sarasota, Florida, where he graduated from Ringling School of Art. His illustrations are done in acrylics and clearly reflect his fine art skills.

STEPHEN MARCHESI has illustrated numerous picture books, textbooks and magazines. A graduate of Pratt Institute, his books have been on the Children's Book Council bestsellers list and on the Bank Street College Children's Book of the Year lists. He lives with his wife and son in Croton-on-Hudson, New York.